GHOUL WARNING
AND OTHER OMENS

BRIAN LUMLEY

Publication Information

A Cry At Night. *Midnight Fantasies*, No. (?) Pre-1977, (Written in 1968).

A Dreamer. *Fantasy & Terror* #5, 1985.

Author! Author! *Astral Dimensions*, No. 6, 1979.

Black Prayer. *Eerie Country*, No. 5, 1981.

City Out of Time. *Fantasy Tales*, Vol. 1, No. 2, Winter 1977.

Da Vinci's Ghost. *Royal Military Police Journal*, the 3rd Quarter, 1975.

Destiny. *Weirdbook*, No. 11, 1977.

Dylath-Leen. In the fanzine Kadath, Vol. 2, No. 1, July 1982.

Enough. *The Arkham Collector*, No. 8, Winter 1971.

Escape. *Escape*, No. 1, Fall, 1977.

Fantasy Crossroads. *Fantasy Crossroads*, Nos. 10/11, March 1977.

Fantasy Tales. *Fantasy Tales*, Vol. 2, No. 3, Summer 1978.

In Pressure-Pounded Chasms. *The Arkham Collector*, No. 9, Spring 1971.

Kadath. In the Brian Lumley Special Edition *Kadath*, Vol. 1, No. 3, November 1980.

Maggot. *Nyctalops*, Vol. 3, No. 1, #15, January 1980.

Mammoth Rider. *Crypt of Cthulhu*, Vol. 3, No. 3 (whole number 19), Candlemas 1984.

Nyctalops. *Nyctalops*, Vol. 2, No. 6 (whole number 13), May 1977.

Pesh-Tlen. *Nyctalops*, Vol. 2, No. 1 (whole number 8), April 1973. (Written in 1968.)

Sea Fret. *Crypt of Cthulhu*, No. 19, 1984.

Shadow Man, The. *The HPL Supplement*, July 1973.

Skull of H. P. L., The. *Weirdbook*, No. 12, 1977.

Swamp Call. *Fantasy Tales*, Vol. 4, No. 8, Summer 1981.

The Wind-Walker. *Fantasy Tales*, Vol. 3, No. 6, Summer 1980.

Tindalos. *Nyctalops*, Vol. 2, No. 7, March 1978.

Visions From Aeons ... Dead? *Omniumgathum,* 1976.
Weirdbook. *Weirdbook,* No. 13, 1977.
Whistler. *Eerie Country,* No. 1, 1976.

Ghoul Warning, Spectre Press, 1982. Amber Man, The Dreamer Wakes, Ghoul Warning, Good God!—Goodrod, I Am the Bat, The Immortal Sword, Inmate, Kraken, Last of the Lizards, Loup Garou, Old Houses Know Too Much, The Sea, Mirrors at Midnight, Survivors, Sword, The Unbearable, Warhorse, The Warlord, Witch, Witching Hour, Y'ha-Nthlei.

Dream. *Ghoul Warning and Other Omens...and Other Omens,* W. P. Ganley, Publisher and Necronomicon Press, 1999. **Dream, Foundling.**

Contents

Dedication

To Richard—For saving them.

Introduction

It has taken me many years to find the last of the poems that have not been in any of the previous *Ghoul Warnings* publications. I have found, I believe, all but one. And that's if that *one* even exists as Brian isn't quite sure about it…after all it was fifty years or more…and you can't remember everything. This poem would be *Mad Dreamer* (?)

In the Acrostics you will find: *Fantasy Crossroads, Pesh-Tlen, The Skull of HPL* and *Maggot.* In Odds and Ends you will find: *A Dreamer.*

Anyway, I have done my best to put this together in electronic form…which all of you know that means having to type the whole thing. But it will satisfy me to finally have the additional missing poems in this edition. This took many hours of my time not including all the work Crossroad Press had to do to get this into an E-format.

And please, I tried to avoid typos but that's not always possible.

I hope you will enjoy this last effort.

Barbara Ann Lumley
Torquay, Devon, UK
2024

Introduction

It's a weird, weird world. The least of my books is the rarest and the most sought after by collectors. The "least" not only because it's a very slim volume but also because it's a book of "poetry," and I can't claim to be a poet any more than I could claim to be a watchmaker—no way! I have difficulty even *winding* my watch. And if I claimed to be a poet…well, I know it would be disputed, and rightly so, because it can so easily be proved that I don't know a damn thing about poetry! No sir, I only know what sounds right to me.

On *The Johnny Carson Show,* Ray Charles talked about people seeing him in his recording studio, wondering how Ray, a blind man, could see all the coloured lights on the console and know what they were doing. "See, I don't care what they're doing!" Ray says "All I know is when it sounds right to me, then it's right." Or words to that effect. And I suppose where poetry is concerned, I'm much the same.

When the first edition of *Ghoul Warning* appeared from Jon Harvey's amateur publishing-house Spectre Press in 1982, over 30 years ago at present date of 2024 for this edition, I could never have imagined the day would come when I would see copies selling for $250.00, or more. I think Jon gave me twenty copies of the hardbound edition, and maybe the same number paperbound. Anyone who dropped in for the next couple of months after that went away with a copy, gratis, signed by myself and Dave Carson the artist, and eventually I had one left. I still have it. Just the one (sob!)…

But poetry…? Several things I did ended up in the wastepaper basket. In fact, whole lot of stuff. I'm talking about stuff I was doing back in the mid-60s to late 70s. And without saying anything to me, my son Richard kept pulling these crumpled balls of paper from the wastebasket. He saved a couple of stories that way too.

iii

But in 1980 when Jon Harvey wanted to do a poetry collection, I just didn't have enough of the things to make a book...or so I thought. Until Richard said, "Yes, you do." Out came these ex-crumpled balls, now badly creased sheets that he'd kept flattened in an old atlas. But there were still a few titles I remembered that I no longer had the words for, except maybe the themes and last lines. So I re-wrote them, and the re-writes went into *Ghoul Warning*. And years later...what do you know? The originals turned up—don't ask me how. Later, in this book, you can read what I've done with them.

Anyway, because Richard had saved them, I dedicated that first, somewhat smaller edition to him—the same reason I'll do it again with this edition.

I've said I don't know anything about poetry except what sounds right to me. That's true. So when in his introduction to Lin Carter's *Dreams from R'lyeh* L. Sprague de Camp talks about him and Carter arguing Fixed-form versus Free-form, I actually envy them that they knew what they were talking about! For at best, I have only a vague idea. It's the same with my writing fiction I suppose. I'm short on theory and long on action—I don't talk about it, I do it. And I don't much think about it when I'm doing it, either. It's in me and has to be out, that's all.

Which is one of the reasons why so-called "critical analysis" of fiction annoys me. I mean, if the writer doesn't know how he did it or what its "hidden meaning" is, how can anyone else? I consider my finest critics to be the three million plus people who have bought my books. They don't *care* what the gurus and petty reviewers—those jittery feverish little lights on the console that do nothing but strobe to the music—are saying; if it reads right to them, it's what they'll buy. The simple fact is that if those gurus, those self-important, brightly coloured flashing lights, could do anything else, then they'd be doing it. I suspect that many a wannabe writer has ended up as a "critical analyst," like a spoiled child on a beach whose sandcastle comes out the wrong shape…so he goes around kicking in everyone else's.

But all that's about *fiction*, which I can talk about with some small measure of justification. But not about poetry. For where poetry is concerned—knowing nothing about it—I must simply accept the judgment of others…

On that point, however:

At *Nikolai's Roof*, a famous eatery in Atlanta, Silky and I were entertained one night by Tom Doherty and Bob Gleason. Both of these fellows know their poetry…I mean they *know* it! Tom at the time was the boss at Tor Books and Bob was his top editor. Starting with ice-cold peach vodka, we quickly moved on to wine, cognacs—oh, and other things. The food was out of this world, and the mood was right. The evening mellowed.

Tom mentioned a poem he'd composed for a loved one; we all demanded to hear it. It was a beautiful thing; but when they're from the heart they always are. Bob followed with a marvelous, heroic piece by one of his favorite, and famous, poets—but don't ask me who because I don't know anything about it. Silky thought it wonderful to feel so good and to be entertained so richly…but these two fellows were now looking at me.

So to make something of a contrast I said: Here's a very small, very sad thing:

"When the din of the battle was over I found
The mount of a warlord, a-lathered but sound.
His hooves were as red as the ground where he stood,
On a mound of the dead, in a valley of blood…"

And so it went, at a gallop, to the end.

When I was done Bob said: "Kipling!"

"What? I'd never Kipled in my life! Tom opined it was by some equally famous poet. But it wasn't, and you can read the rest of *Warhorse* in this book. I didn't care what the coloured lights were doing as long as it sounded right. And quite obviously it did.

Sounding right, it made my night. If only a few more of them had come out that way.

As for why this book is still a slim one—and that despite the fact that it's a handful of poems longer than the first book—and even longer in this edition of five more poems found—it's the fault of that old wastepaper basket, and the fact that Richard (my son) wasn't around more of the time but Silky (Barbara Ann) was around for those five new ones in this edition. Also, it dawned on me a long time ago that poetry wasn't my scene; I just couldn't afford to throw away all these storylines on bits of doggerel.

And I can't afford it in more senses than one. Not least in wasted time, which I never have enough of in the first place. You see, no one ever got rich writing poetry (or short stories, or letters for that matter, as witness Lovecraft), which is why I write novels: because I have to earn my keep. Oh, I suppose I *will* still write the odd short story, when I have a really good idea that demands I work on it, or just to keep my hand. But I'm sorry—or maybe I'm not—this one is definitely the first and last of my poetry. No more new rhyming from me.

Brian Lumley
Devon
February 2023

Briefly

At a long-ago Fantasy or Horror convention in America—I can't remember which—the infamous Darrell Schweitzer challenged me to write a limerick rhyming his name. Sounds utterly impossible, right?

So I went away and came back ten minutes later with this:

For Darrell:
I've just read a story by Schweitzer
By golly, it gave me a fright sir!
It's about this young gel
Who falls down a well,
Where a Burrower rears up and bites her!

Not to be outdone, Darrell at once remarked: "You do realize that's now part of the Cthulhu Mythos, don't you?"

Well, well!

Brian Lumley
Devon
February 2023

Acrostics

Some of these were written out of my admiration for Lovecraft's Cthulhu Mythos, others for the fun of it, and a handful for the fanzines of the day such as *Weirdbook, Kadath, Fantasy Tales,* and *Escape*. The only poem I ever wrote that doesn't rhyme is also in this batch; *Nyctalops*, written for Harry O. Morris's excellent, now sadly defunct, 'zine of the same name.

In *Fantasy Tales* there's a small error in the last line; indeed, it's the very last word. My first wife, Gail was very much on my mind at the time it was written. The word should be "gales" obviously. But in fact there were two "Gails," for it's my eldest daughter's name, too. Perhaps that's how this came to be…and perhaps we are occasionally subconsciously guided in the things we write after all. Oddly enough, the error wasn't picked up by the magazine *Fantasy Tales*, and it was missed again when a book, *The Best of Fantasy Tales*, appeared several years later!

Well, I'm not going to mess with fate. So Gail (or gails) it is…

B.L.

Fantasy Crossroads

Fiends of hell and warriors bold,
Ancient sorceries, towers of gold,
Nighted crypts where tales are told
To chill the blood of demons fell.
Awful magicks fill each page,
Swords flash from a bygone age,
Young bloods face a mighty mage,
Challenging his every spell.
Reavers rage and roar their wrath,—
Olden runes obscure their path,—
Still they cleave a bloody swath,
Sending all their foes to hell.
Raging monsters from the deeps
Of primal oceans guard the keeps
And sepulchres where star-spawn sleeps,
Drowned since time long gone—
So, my friend, **read on**…!

Pesh-Tlen

But what vile Gods of chance have I none fouled
That such a fate is mine, I who have known,
The lore of dark dimensions and have prowled,
Along strange sea-beds fearless and alone.
I—who have trod the vault between the motes
Which men call stars—I who saw time begin—
Who have known praise from ululating throats
Who Dagon in his might has named his kin.
That this, this horror is the will of HE,
Who lies in Deep Gill—Ho I know full well,
But why did grinning unkind faith choose me,
In such an awful habitat to dwell?
That I should have to feature in HIS plan,
Imprisoned in the body of a man.

The Skull of HPL

Temple of Shrieking Fear—
Wherein dead dark Lords
Born of lost dimensions loom,
And great alien shapes leer,
Utterly void of Earth-born tomb,
 —How is it that vastly sepulchres of dread,
 Brim-filled with nightmares of the unquiet dead,
 Were housed…in this one author's head?

Maggot

M ealy-mouthed gnawer of Death's damp rot,
A wesome your power, Eater of Men:
G reat warriors may not deny you,
G houls alone might defy you,
O h, but briefly, so briefly, and then...
T hey also are yours, Lord Maggot!

Nyctalops

Nighted chasms of dream and legend
Yawn within kraken-devised
Covers; tottering Cimmerian towers and
Tumbled R'lyehan ruins whisper their secrets,
Ancient monolith and drowned, dreaming sepulchre.
Lovecraftian horrors loom leeringly,
Opening gates to spheres best forgotten. Ho!—
Pharaos in Fandomic gloom,
Shine on, light in the night of legends.

The Warlord

Towering, stern of eye and hand,
Heavy-browed and iron-thewed,
Enemies fall before your breath.
Warrior-king whose every mood
And whim is echoed o'er the land,
Rude of strength, of power rude:
Lord of armies, Minister of Death.
Old in the skills of war, with blood imbru'd,
Ride on, with steed of steel at your command—
Doom's drum pounds in your pulsing blood!

Tindalos

Time's angles, mages tell, conceal a place
Incredible, beyond the mundane mind:
Night-shrouded and *outside* the seas of space,
Doomed Tindalos blows on the ageless wind.
And where the black and corkscrew towers climb,
Lost and athirst the ragged pack abides,
Old as the aeons, trapped in tombs of time,
Sailing the tortuous temporal tides…

Dylath-Leen

Down where the Southern Sea meets
    tinkling Skai,
      I woke, my boat breached gently on
        the strand,
Yawned sleep's dull sloth from mind
    and from my eye brushed fading
    visions of the waking land.
Lo, it was evening, and behind the bay,
    a darkling city all devoid of light
And gaunt in silhouette against the ray
    of failing sunlight beckoned on the night.
Tall rose the towers of that lightless town,
    black were the wharves that echoed
    to my tread,
Hag-eyed, the broken windows peered down
upon me as from faces of the dead.

Long gone the fishers from that fearsome fane
    of evil...aye, long gone all honest men,

Escaped the peril seeped from lands insane
    and brought in galleys black from
    leering Leng.
Even as I knew the place it seemed I heard the
    whining flutes of things obscene;
Ne'er looking back I ran, and ran, and screamed—
    pursued by all the ghosts of Dylath-Leen...

Fantasy Tales

Forgotten lands of time-lost lore
Astound the senses, lifting high
Nacreous towers to a sky
That dreamers swear they've known
    Before—of yore.
And warriors grim ride mighty steeds,
Sore pressed by runes of devilish source,
Yet never once avoid the course
That augers destinies of deeds—and dooms.
And galleons with scarlet sails
Loom out of misted oceans deep;
Ensorcelled oarsmen, fast asleep,
Said on through sun and rain and gails
—in Fantasy-Tales!

The Wind-Walker

(In dreams I converse with Him, and ask:)

Weird wanderer of interstellar ways,
Ice-God of frigid-flamed auroral skies,
Nightmare Lord whose glaring gorgon gaze
Dooms all who see into your carmine eyes:
Whence came you here, why, how long ago,
Anthropomorphic god of Esquimaux?

(He answers:)
Long aeons gone, before Man's watery birth,
Kthulhut the Master brought us down to Earth;
Even the cinder-stars burst into flame,
Rejoicing when at last we Old Ones came!

Kadath

Kadath has called to me from dreams gone by,
And now in answer to that call I stand
Alone beneath a lowering, leaden sky,
Atop Leng's plateau in the cold wasteland.
Depressed my spirit, fearful my shade,
Which wanders now in primal Sarkomand,
And pauses on a ruined esplanade
Before a giant-carven basalt hand.
The way is plain, the finger points the path,
And now a tittering Shantak bids me ride–
How far across the Cold Waste to Kadath?
To onyx castle – and what waits inside!

Escape!

Entombed in plastic entropy,
Sunken in ruts of toil,
Condemned to faltering Earth
And one short mortal coil–?
Peruse the magic page and flee life's rape:
Escape, escape, escape, escape!

Entrapped in ugly mold,
Soulless, dispirited and bound–
Confined to mundane spheres, lost
And seldom found–?
Perhaps we'll yet spring up from, naked ape:
Escape, escape, escape, ESCAPE!

Weirdbook

Words of horror, poison dipped,
Echo from a nameless crypt–
Insane, bereft of mind.
Rare blooms sway in moldering beds,
Darkly hissing hybrid heads
Bloat in caverns blind.
Only let my slumbers be,
Only keep from smoth'ring me,
Kthulhut's spells that bind.

Y'ha-Nthlei

Your name is strange to land-born ears—
How weird the sound, like rolling tides—
And visions conjured: of sunken
    sepulchre and tomb.
None but the Deep Ones know the years
Turned to aeons since pre-dawn ides,
Hideously primal, birthed a monster
    from its womb
Leering out of vaults of space; or the fears
Evinced by His Temple, sunken where
the dolphin rides.
In Y'ha-Nthlei, crab-crowned,
    Cthulhu's idol glooms.

Stories

In my introduction I mentioned that a lot of these verses were short stories that didn't develop beyond doggerel. Well here they are. Any changes I've made are minimal—but no matter how I work them I know some of them will never sound quite right. Not any longer. I have a different ear now, that's all...

My personal favorite of these, and probably my favorite of all my "poems," is the first one, *City Out of Time*.

But there's one other that's worth a mention, if only because I discovered it at the last moment in Randy Everts' *Etching's and Odysseys*, No. 9, 1986—but God only knows how long Randy had had it!—that had been mislaid, overlooked, or just plain simply forgotten. I am talking about *Dream*, which only came to light when I was looking for something else entirely. So here it is, if only to make this book as complete as I know how.

B.L.

City Out of Time

Betrayed by dreams I wander weirdling ways,
Beneath the fronds of palms in jungles old
When Earth herself was young and brave and bold.
Where hybrid blooms sway serpentine I gaze
On ruins which no other eyes have seen,
Whose black foundations sink in primal green,
A-crawl with efts of prehistoric days.

Beyond odd-angled ruins ceaseless pound
The waves of frenzied ocean freshly borned,
Which never yet Man's ancestor have spawned,
And here I find strange mysteries profound:
These monoliths of which I stand in awe—
Who builded them upon this ancient shore?
And what wild secrets have the ages drowned?

From books in waking worlds I know the name
Of such a city lost in ocean deep,
Where Ancient Ones in unquiet slumbers keep
The lore of dark dimensions and the flame
Of elder magicks burning, 'til a time
When upward from the aeon-silted slime
Vast shapes will come—as once before they came.

Aye, and that fane of evil was R'lyeh,
Where dreaming Cthulhu lies in chains that bind,
Sending his nightmares out to humankind,
Drowning their noble dreams in nameless mire.
And dreaming still I start as from the pile
Snake tentacular arms and in a while—
A *face* that crowns the bulk of Evil's Sirel

Amber Man

They found him washed in salt and sand,
With open eye, however glazed,
Cast up upon the ocean's strand,
In amber trapped, in death amazed.

Full fifty million years gone by
Since last the sun shone in his face;
Where did he come from? How, and why?
This man—attired in suit of space!

Enough

Enough, tonight when she returns I will
Speak to her of the wrong she does my name;
While I lie here, incapable and ill,
She's out pursuing her licentious game.
With friend or foe I know not but I fear,
That while my illness lingers day by day,
I lose her more, the one I hold most dear,
That with her lover she might fly away!

Or is it all illusion—all a lie—?
The errands which she runs: are they for me?
That devil jealousy—to think that I
Distrust her clean and pure fidelity.
The creaking stair, the door, at last my wife
Returns to me—but why that wicked knife?

A Cry at Night

That sound—despair, frustration intertwined,
The loneliness of the abode reflected,
Impinging on my being, on my mind—
The crying of my cat, all day neglected.
He sallied forth this morning, still unfed,
To search the nearby wilds for some fair She,
And now, so late, it seems that Hunger's led
Old Tom back home that he may now woo me.

My tale can wait—I throw my pen aside.
He howls so strange, perhaps Old Tom is hurt.
A lesson to you, Tom, who can't abide
Beside the hearth but must go out to flirt.
I fling the door wide, laughing—but out there
…It is not Tom who crouches on the stair!

Sea Fret

It's the sea fret I fear, for it tells me
That the evening is nigh and the tide
Will soon at the rear of the old
    rotting pier—
And my woman is not by my side.

It's the mist on the ocean that chills me,
With a chill that I cannot abide,
For the wavelets that race seem to form
    the sad face—
Of the woman who once was my bride.

T'was an evening like this we argued,
And I struck her so hard that she cried,
And she fell from the rear of the old
    rotting pier—
And was taken away by the tide.

Now the mist it rolls up off the ocean,
And to greet it I throw my arms wide;
Then—that soul-wrenching smell
    as she steps up from hell!
And once more she is there by my side…

Old Houses Know Too Much

Old houses know too much,
About the people who
Have lived in them, as such
They're dangerous! And you,
Old house, are particularly so,
For *she* lived in you, with me;
And looking at you I know
You loved her. So you see—
I've really no choice
But to set touch
To you with fire. Your voice
Is roaring flame—you know too much!

You hear her screams
From behind fresh bricks,
Shared her last dreams,
Felt her final, spastic kicks,
And lately, in my bed,
I've felt your chill. No doubt
You'd like to see me dead…
So burn—but first, God!—let *me* out!

Survivors

We crouched within the cellar's dusky gloom
While evening crept across the land outside.
And cursed the fates that made us run and hide
With bated breath within this lightless tomb.

The old man shivered in his rags and said:
"By God—if God there be—what did we do?
We were the Lords of Earth, oh yes, it's true!"
And then he sobbed and hung his greying head.

"Quiet, old man," I whispered, "and no harm
Will come to you. They have no sight as such."
"Ah, young friend, you don't remember much!"
He answered, and he touched my trembling arm.

"You must have been a child when they
        crushed Man,
No more than three or four at most, I'd guess
Who would have thought that this unholy mess
Could come about in one short lifetime's span?"

But then a sharp *hiss* sounded from on high,
And I backed off and heard the old man scream,
And then—(dread nightmare I shall always dream),
I saw that *thing* reach down, and watched him die!

In Pressure-Pounded Chasms

I

Beneath the yacht the bell was fast descending
Toward unfathomed deeps of silent gloom,
While on the deck the crew and I were lending
A hand with cables and the pulley-boom.
Thornton was anxious, to his tasks attending,
Coaxing his precious switches, dials and all;
His sharp instructions seemingly unending,
Controlling his deep-diving camera's fall.

Maloney, from *The Times*, was busy making
Notes for his column, silent for a while.
"Five thousand fathoms—better start the braking."
Cried Thornton, and we slowed the deep missile.
"There's little changed down there since time began;
We'll see it soon—if all goes to my plan."

II

"Now hold it and I'll get the camera started
Before we let the cable out some more;
I've got so far I don't want to be thwarted
By smashing it upon the ocean floor."
He twiddled with his dials and on the screen
A picture of the deeps began to show:
Strange fish the like of which we'd never seen
Went ogling by with luminescent glow.

"A bit more line," cried Thornton,

"But be gentle;
I only pray the brakes can take the load…"
Upon his face, for all to see, the menta!
Strain he was undergoing plainly showed…
While in the depths the bell moved all serene
Through abysses of Noden's dark demesne.

III

All were aware of Thornton's fear of failing
And knew the brilliant man's avowed intent;
He'd told us all, before we started sailing,
Of his one dread—unwanted sediment!
He wished to see the rocks as they'd once been,
Before Time wreaked its havoc on the land,
And hoped the deepest ocean floor was clean,
Not buried underneath soft-silted sand.

It seemed to me the screen showed his success
As wide expanses floated into view,
Of stretching plains and rocky wilderness;
Of unexplored horizons, old yet new.
Then, in amazed excitement, Thornton swore
At something else which suddenly he saw.

IV

For there, imprinted on the solid stone—
Laid down by what or when no one could say—
Were monstrous prints of something quite
    unknown,
As though fresh made in Cretaceous clay.
"Who would have thought," I whispered

then in awe,
"That there would be such traces way
    down there?
A sight no man has ever seen before—
A secret of the past at last laid bare."

Then with a *crack!* The pulley brake-burst free,
And on the screen the view loomed quickly close.
The bell rushed to the bottom of the sea
But did not smash…old Thornton's features
    froze.
"Great Scott!" he whispered then. "It
    can't be true!
That bed's not rock—it's mud. *Those
    prints are new!"*

Whistler

A lonely road all misted gloom,
Distorted by the shapes of night,
And shadowed trees that leer and loom
To fill the heart with fright.

A mile to go and then one more
Before I knock with trembly fist
Upon the hidden, unmarked door
And greet the one I've missed.

To keep my darkling fears at bay,
I whistle as I pass along,
A tuneless tune along the way,
The way that seems so long.

And then, befriended by the moon,
Which cleaves the clouds to light my path,
I whistle a less breathless tune
And tread the silver swath.

Then dark once more and more afraid,
I whistle louder while the road
Seems even longer through the glade,
And heavier my load.

But then I snort at my own fears
And fondly pat my weighty swag,
To think a ghoul of all my years
Should fear what's in his bag!

The Immortal Sword

In my youth?—Ah, the world was much grander,
When bright cities were strewn on the land,
And a blood such as I would not pander
To the rebuffs of god, friend or man.
There were wars to be won, pride was taken
In the chop of an axe well swung,
Or the back of a foe neatly braken—
Now I'm old, but my sword is still young.

There were women to love—ha, such beauties!
And the ale ran like water in flood,
And a lover would not shirk his duties,
When his payment was so very good.
I remember the Black Raiders coming, how my
    Woman lay dead where she clung
To my breast, and this sword of mine humming—

Now…I'm old, but the sword is still young.
There was blood in my eyes and the roaring
Of red blood in my ears as I stood,
And it sent my young heart's black rage soaring,
And my blade was a scythe of bright blood…!
In the dawn the tribe stood disbelieving,
Of the berserker song we had sung,
And they found me beside my love, grieving—
Now I'm old, but my sword is still young.

Dream

Once while wandering home by night
Something made me start in fright,
Set my soul to fearsome flight
   —I, too, in terror fled;

I saw strange universes reeling,
Heard mad clappers wildly pealing,
Felt an unknown alien feeling,
   Dreams and nightmares wed.

Parallel worlds opened before me,
In obeisance things adored me,
Shades of madness fought to claw me
   'Til my nerve ends bled.

When the lunacy had passed,
I returned to Earth at last,
Finding my feet flying fast
   From a hideous dread;

Home again great peals of thunder
Greeted me in awesome wonder,
On my bell all torn asunder
   I was lying dead.

Loup Garou

What's that you say?—repeat that date…
My God! You're sure? Oh, no!
And look, the hour—so very late—
And the village lights aglow.

But no time to curse and wonder
How it's come around so soon,
For I've made a dreadful blunder,
And…just look!—*the Rising moon!*

It creeps above the mountain high,
And in its deadly ray,
There's just one thing that's certain: I
Must live in hell 'til day!

No use to stand there gaping, no,
Run!—Quick!—Get out of town!
Just one last thing before you go:
For God's sake—*strap me down!*

Last of the Lizards

The mist was low and the drums beat slow
As the marching men drew nigh,
And the morning star seemed to gloat afar
On the fate of the men,
Of the brave fighting men —
On the fare of the men who would die.

There was blood on the sun and its colour was dun
As it rose in the distant east.
By its dull distant gleam they could see in the stream
Their grim mirror eyes —
Their narrow grey eyes —
As they gazed on the land of the beast.

For over the ford where the boglands swelled broad
A batrachian horde lay in wait,
Green-webbed were their hands and they envied
    the lands
Of these daring young men
Who would enter the fen,
Of the men who came on to their fate.

For by night the cold beast would foray and feast
On the warm vibrant blood of the clan,
So the creeping green horde must be put to the sword,
Must be crushed to the last —
Feel the withering blast —
Of the hatred of clean-limbed Man.

In the slime and the muck, with their forked tongues
    they struck,

As they fell from the moss-festooned trees,
But the lads from the clan, they fought back to a man,
And their eyes were now red
As they heaped lizard dead,
As dead leaves are heaped by a breeze.

When the sun stood on high in the azure blue sky
Through the cooling clean waters they bore.
Of the hundred and eight who had challenged their fate.
Only twelve now remained—
And of these three were maimed—
But the lizard-man threat was no more.

From the pages of time there had vanished a line
Whose horror is no longer known
Were it not for the clan…what price now for Man?
What price for this race—
For this great human race—
Would its first seeds have ever been sown?

Sword

They called him Sword, for tall and straight,
His strength was steel, and bright of eye,
He feared not to greet his fate,
With ringing steel-on-steely cry.

Aye, men may come and men may go,
But now and then one like a Lord
Will win his way, and blow by blow,
Will earn himself a name like Sword.

For barbarous his clan and wild,
Bred of the grey Cimmerian scene,
Where Sword grew up from sturdy child
To iron man of stern demean.

But in the end all men are dust,
And all must die when brain is gored,
When blood like iron turns to rust—
A battle lost—a broken Sword.

Foundling

Picked up off the doorstep, he didn't look a lot—
Blue with the cold, with eyes too old, the bolt
   of life half-shot.

We called him Charlie Nobody, gave him a pick at four.
By God! At ten, he worked with men, and ate a damn
   sight more!

Too late we started wondering, just who has Ma had been;
Too late, and how, because right now he's pushing
   seventeen…

We should have noticed right away, there was never
   any joy
In his ancient eyes—he was just too wise
   —For a *human* baby boy!

Swamp Call

There was blood on the moon last evening,
And a mist that hung low on the moor,
And the sea-fret appeared to be weaving
A dance that was dismal and dour.

I could tell by such signs what was coming:
Strange times when I'd feel the swamp's lure,
When the wind in the reeds would be humming
A song that was dank and impure.

For my love lies in rushes and mire,
Where I laid her the night that she died,
The same night that my brain burst with fire
And red rage when I found how she'd lied!

There was blood on the moon last evening,
And a sad voice that called through the mist
To tell me my lost love was grieving,
That her lips fondly longed to be kissed.

So I'll leave my drear cot when the owl calls,
And I'll cleave for the swamp in the night,
And you'll hear a small splash as the mist falls,
And her arms close about me so tight…

Mammoth Rider

Reincarnated, I dream of days long gone,
Before Man's cities sprawled across the land,
When in an earlier world I was the one
The tribes adored and called the Mammoth Man.

For as a pup I'd found a pachyderm
More young than I, forsaken by the herd,
Which would have died had I not kept the germ
Of life secure with money and goat curd.

And so we grew together, mighty-thewed,
And legended by each and every clan
Who saw the man-child riding on a rude
Great beast…and called him Mammoth Man.

And young and strong we wandered all the ways
Of that primeval world, and knew the joy
Of freedom and adventure, and our days
Were glad together—beast and human boy.

But fate must overcome and in the end,
Bemired in jungle swamp of morass glue,
The mighty creature I had called my friend
Expires at last, and I—why, I died, too…

Warhorse

When the din of the battle was over I found
The mount of a warlord, a-lathered but sound.
His hooves were as red as the ground where he stood,
On a mound of the dead, in a valley of blood.

And he pawed at his master and gave a wild cry,
As if to say: "Lord, this is no place to die!"
But his master was gone and the wound in his head
Spoke of life that was done, of a spirit well fled.

As I caught at his bridle he whinnied and reared,
And baring his teeth stood red-eyed and flat-eared.
Then—great beast that he was—he just stood there
    and cried,
And he laid down beside his old master and died.

If I'm ever a warlord of legended deed,
Crom grant me the love of just such a steed!

Shadow Man

Once while wandering through dark
    midnight streets
And pausing in an ill-lit thoroughfare
Where all about felt thick with hell's efreets,
I felt upon my back a sudden stare;
A look so piercing I was filled with dread,
That someone could direct so vile a glare
Upon my person—so I turned my head,
And saw, high in a garret, someone there.

"I seek a room," I called. "It grows so late,
Would you allow me, sir, to share your board?
Tonight the very air seems filled with hate—
It's certainly no night to be abroad…"
He beckoned me to climb in wormy gloom
To the high turrets of his garret room.

"You're welcome," came the whisper
    through the door,
"To share my room—though first I
    must explain—
I dwell in darkness, for my eyes are sore
From some strange photophobia's morbid pain.
Before you enter—douse the landing light,
And then I'll bid you welcome to my room;
For I swear, sir, I could not bear the sight
Of that dread brightness, I who dwell in gloom."

I did as bade, and as the door swung wide
My host stood in the doorway silhouetted;
I stepped within—and knew that he had lied—

40

And nameless fear at my innards fretted.
He led me to a stool and then sat where
He once more might observe the thoroughfare.
Against the wall I rested my tired frame,
And then, unthinking, filled my rose-wood bowl.
Unconsciously, I swear, I struck the flame
Which thrust the shadows back in that dark hole.
My host, he screamed and struck aside my hand,
And cursed that he had dared to take me in,
Knowing that I now must understand
The horrifying state that he was in.

Frozen in awe I sat as he explained
In frenzied speech the terror I had seen,
How from his being some warlock had drained
An integer of what he once had been.
Aloud then, in that room, I sat and prayed —
My flaring match had shown he cast no shade!

My disbelieving ears heard his tale
Of how within that city there did dwell
Somewhere a man who'd seen behind the veil
And learned the secrets of a nameless hell.
He told of how this being owned a tome,
Which bore no word but carried on each leaf
A shadow-blot whose indigenous home
Was some poor recluse driven thus to grief.

"The shadow is the very soul, my friend.
Without it, man is merely a sad shell.
I curse the fiend who brought me to this end,
That in eternal darkness I must dwell.
I sit here with my rifle through each day,
And pray that he might once more pass my way."

Then, as he finished speaking, he did take
Down from the wall a cared-for weapon which
He sighted from the window 'ere he spake—
And suddenly his whispering voice grew rich:
"He comes, I know it, stalking through the night.
I sense him, as for years I've dreamed I would;
And I have been appointed to put right
The wrong's he's done—he'll pay his debts in blood!"

I could not move—he tensed and aimed his shot,
But not into the darkened street below;
There came a deafening blast—and then a blot
Of something dark across the floor did flow.
As sudden moonlight came I gibbering fled—
The spreading shadow at his feet was red!

Odds and Ends

This final section is composed of odds and ends. Two of the pieces, *The Sea* and *Da Vinci's Ghost*, have no macabre connection whatsoever; but the sea has always fascinated me, and I used to fly hang-gliders all over Scotland's Pentland Hills, as for *Witch*, of the least of these pieces: it was probably one of the first I wrote way back when I was fourteen or fifteen, for a British fanzine of the time, called *Nezfez* if I remember correctly. But that was (God!) sixty years ago. First and last, as it now works out...

Inmate and *Destiny* are interesting in that they are two of the poems I considered lost. (That old wastepaper basket again.) But copies did survive to find their way into the amateur press magazines *Weirdbook* and *Etchings and Odysseys*. Meanwhile, remembering the titles and the last lines, I had re-written them. Each version tells the same story but in a different way! Now, by joining them up, I've simply made the story longer. The first fourteen lines of *Destiny* are from *Etchings and Odysseys* and the second set from *Weirdbook*. Neither version was in the original *Ghoul Warning*. In *Inmate*, the second set of fourteen lines originally appeared in *Etchings*, while the first set was in *Ghoul Warning*! Confused? Don't be—just read them.

To finish off, this last section of verse is followed by my original Preface.

B.L.

43

A Dreamer

Having retired late, after reading Fantasy & Terror!

Forbidden runes describe age
Awesome in its mysteries,
Naming continents and seas
That know a strange and alien rage.
Ancient scrolls prescribe that time
Sorcerers and peril-fraught
Yarns of wizards, devil-brought.

And heroes bold or spun in rhyme.
Nighted castles tower where
Dooms and deadly terrors loom;

Torturous labyrinths of gloom
Echo monstrous laughter there…
Reeking lakes of horror roll,
Roil in caverns of the mind,
O Lord, I beg thee, pray unbind,
Release my dreaming soul!

Ghoul Warning

You've probably sensed them in graveyards,
Where headstones lean, thick with grey mould;
Though they're not as many now, mainly diehards,
Still their race is as wise as it's old.

It's best to be keen-eyed and wary—
If you must delve around, not alone;
Such things are at best, you know—scary,
And some like their meat on the bone!

And the thing is, you can't hear them coming—
Not a sound but your own heart-beat's knell,
Or the wind in the trees weirdly humming—
You won't *hear* them…but you'll know their smell!

The Sea

The sea has a magnet's hold on me:
By night, when the moon is round,
I stand by the strand and the things I see
In my dreaming mind's eye, 'twixt the sea and the sky,
Are things which are seldom found.

The sea has the lure of the Lorelei,
And its wash is a Siren's rhyme,
And the sound of its waves might be a sigh—
Or the rush and the roar of the waters that pour
Down the Cataracts of Time...

The sea is the start and the end of me,
And its rhythm is the rhythm of my soul;
For its spirit is willful, wild and free,
And its pulse is so vast that its future and past,
Are as one—and I'm part of that whole.

Da Vinci's Ghost

(As seen through the eyes of a hang-gliding Enthusiast.)

Ah, Leonardo —
If only you had known,
For you had enough bravado,
And the field was all your own.

No other fool was trying,
The skies were high and wide,
Only the birds were flying...
Perhaps that's why you tried?

But for all your string and parchment,
Your feathers and your glue,
This was the one department
That baffled even you.

Yet now it often seems to me,
When I'm soaring all alone,
That your grey ghost sits beside me,
And I hear you gently groan:

"I had the right idea." You say,
"But my wings were much too small —
And I couldn't seem to find the way —
And those feathers ruined it all!"

Then, when you've done with crying,
Why! — your shade seems more at ease,
For now, at last, you're flying!
— Like a feather on the breeze.

Witching Hour

Hour of midnight, Noon's dark opposite,
Strikes on the still, chill air,
Each peal a mist-muted composite
Of giant's pulse, staccato cry from lair
Of nameless beast.

Twelve—and the giant dies…
The air is breathless and the chill
Of night bites deep, and chittering cries
Swell loud and close—*be still!*—
They come to feast!

Author! Author!

If time is but a sloughing off of Life,
And Life itself a dreary, drawn-out play,
As we are Extras whose eternal Strife
Can only take us closer, day by day,
Toward the final curtain-call named Death—
Then tell me: when the theatre lights go down,
And all the Actors breathe their final breath,
And mummied audience to ghostly town retreats...
What Power will pen the Opus after that?
The Quill of God—or tooth of coffin-rat?

Inmate

Though you assure me I have dwelled too long
Upon strange things which do not bear recall,
And tell me that the hideous hunting throng
Which seeks my soul does not exist at all,
I say to you that you have never seen
The like of those who haunt my dreams at night,
For then you, too, would soon have fled the scene
Or such a horror, gibbering in fright.

It is not hard for you to say my mind
Is ill and needs to rest and must not dwell
Upon those things which only seek to bind
Me to my own multi-dimensional hell.
I *laugh* at you who have not heard the calls
Of those who dwell behind these padded walls!

Your voices, reassuring and warm,
With human kindness brimming in each word,
Decry the things I know that I have heard
And view my "crazy fancies" with alarm.
The mind (you say) is hard to understand,
With secret, sunken places deep inside,
Where such as I retreat and try to hide
When little things don't go as we had planned.

And patiently you work on me each day,
And pride yourselves when I at last agree,
And nod my head and say: "Ah, yes—I see!"
But then, at last, when you all go away—
I laugh at you who have not heard the calls
Of those who dwell BEHIND these padded walls!

51

Destiny

To hear your voices filled with learned phrase
And see the miracles of your design,
One would not guess your aeon a mere phase,
A thickening in a continuous line.
You can plan to span the heavens 'twixt the orbs
Which speed around your tiny, flaring sun,
Mere cosmic moments since you splashed your daubs
On cavern walls when time had just begun.

Believing the whole universe is yours,
You multiply through space—or will do soon—
Not guessing that you merely tread the course
Led onwards by some nameless piper's tune.
Allow me—one who knows—to name your place:
You are the plankton of the seas of space!

You talk about the Destiny of Man,
The rise and fall of Empires, and of Kings
And Queens long turned to mummy-dust, and things
All pre-ordained to fall in with your plan.
A million worlds there are like yours, and aye,
A million races with the same vain drive:
Galactic Empire—conquer, crush, and thrive—
And he who would deny you, let him die!

As if your puny words or works might cause
The smallest ripple in the Cosmic Sea,
The merest leaf upon the Cosmic Tree
To tremble—and what of the Cosmic Laws?
Allow me, one who knows, to name your place:
You are the plankton of the seas of space!

Kraken

Weird-winged beast whose vans have plied the sky
Beyond all lands of human ken and far
Beyond the farthest spheres that swim on high,
Whose eyes have burned on many an alien star—
Why came you here where Man the biped worm,
Rules now where once your word alone was law?
Why rested you upon this world that form
Alhazred in his maddest dreams saw?

Had you but journeyed on then were you free,
To roam the galaxies unto this day—
Instead, you slumber here, beneath the sea,
Where Elder Gods you spawn have locked away.

The Unbearable

I cannot bear the thought of lying still,
Beneath the ground where worms may
    come and go,
And do with me whatever is their will,
And know that I might never say them no…

I cannot bear the thought of earth above,
Of green field overhead where once I passed,
Of teardrops from eyes that sparked with love,
But now must cry for one who breathed his last.

And worse than all of this is the ghastly shroud,
Which compliments the coffin's satin gloom…
I *cannot bear* these things—I shriek aloud,
And mercifully wake…*within my tomb!*

I Am The Bat

I am the bat—silently screaming, I fly,
Dartingly, startling, on membrane wings,
Full in the face of the night sky,
Whose voice, the night wing, sings.
And when the moon, with soft Cycloptic eye,
Peers down upon old roofs where darkness clings,
Like velvet shroud, I fall—
To where she waits, who soon must die…

Visions From Aeons...Dead?

Dreaming visions of pulsing, star-strewn spaces
Unfold in vasty voids whose ancient chill
Has lasted since the Dawn of Time and will
Go on until decay or doom replaces
The throb of Cosmic Life. And in my dreaming,
I seem to hear the very light-years screaming,
As evil seeps from unguessed, nameless places.

For winging down between the constellations
And nebulae of nether-voids I see
Dim, distant shapes whose outlines are to me
The ultimate in Hell's abominations.
Such frothing, shrieking, leaping nightmare spawn!.,
And as they pass, from cinders suns are born,
In madly blazing cosmic conflagrations...

Then, tingling at that sight some inner chord
Is struck—and at the last I start awake,
Shuddering at the shapes my fancies take,
That dreams could propagate that monstrous horde,
But then, beyond my window's frosted glass,
Dimly it seems I see weird phantoms pass—
And then I pray, who never praised the Lord!

The Dreamer Wakes

Nightmare's mire sucks me down
It its tide of horror-dreams;
Deep in chasms of ill-renown
I drift on poisoned streams.
    Lord, I swear I'll never more
    Gorge myself on Horror's fare;
    All my love of Blood and gore
    Ends with this nightmare…
All the nighted tomes I've read,
I shall heap and gladly burn;
All the tales of troubled dead,
Readily I'll spurn…
    Lord, I get thee, let me wake,
    Rouse me up from Hell's own deep;
    Hold me to these vows I make—
    But only break this sleep!
Shocked from dream I start awake,
But…my throat frames one last scream;
Leech-sucked dry in scarlet lake—
God!—*this is no dream!*

Black Prayer

Lord God, whose very Name devours my heart,
If I yet have a soul that You may take,
I pray Thee take it—do not let me start
Awake beneath the thirsty, sharpened stake.

Mirrors At Midnight

Mirrors at midnight frighten me,
When seemingly strange faces leer
From spaces only mine should ever fill;
And images distort until I see
Outlines with eyes that peer,
As if directed by some Other's will.

What is it in glass at night
That sets the heart to pounding?
That strikes the soul as vile?
Perhaps it is only the sight
Of a face which should be frowning—
Giving back a knowing, gnawing smile!
And, to lighten things up a little!

Good God!—Goodrod

Goodrod the Tiny's sword was sharp,
His axe was keen and blue,
And by his boot he hung his lute,
His knife and quiver, too.

With crossbow on one shoulder,
Spiked mace locked to his wrist.
Feeling the strain of steel and chain
He reeled about half-pissed!

In skill-at-arms a master,
He feared not man or god,
(So small was he they could not see
To smite the little sod!)

The moral of this story, girls,
When you're seeking out a mate:
Do not despise a man's small size—
His weapon might be great!

Witch

I heard her wicked eerie shriek
As high above me she did sail,
Saw her cat so black and sleek,
Heard her cloak slap in the gale.

As high above me she did soar,
I saw her eyes burn red and deep,
And prayed I'd see her nevermore—
But still she haunts me in my sleep!

Three "Stories" in 50 Words Each

One...

The Do-it-yourself Carpenter

The idea was to take some six-by-fours, a handful of nails and a little inspiration, and start a craze to change the entire world. Impossible? But he did it! Blood, sweat and tears played their parts—personal sacrifice, you know? They rewarded him with a crown of thorns.

Two...

War of the Worlds II: Earthlings v Pondlings

Ron and Mikh, joining forces, went out to explore space. There they found an alien race: weird shapes, sizes—sexes! Outnumbered, the armies of Ron and Mikh bred and bred, finally defeating their diversified foe. Mankind stood no chance against intelligent amoebas whose single strategy was to divide and conquer.

Three...

Decreation

Monday. Looking down from on high the astronaut gaped. Where was everyone? On Tuesday the animals disappeared; Wednesday, the birds and fishes; Thursday saw sun and stars snuffed, the moon magicked away. Then the trees died, and Saturday was Chaos. But the astronaut had been right. On Sunday God rested.

My Preface (1982) to the Original Book Went Like This:

I suppose I'm lucky to have been an Arkham House acolyte, for Arkham was surely the major source of my sort of verse. Over the years I've read some great fantasy poetry—whimsical, wonderful, stirring stuff. Such as *Dark of the Moon* and *Fire and Sleet and Candlelight;* and Clark Ashton Smith's, H. P. Lovecraft's, de Camp's and Wandrei's books. Great stuff! I've always wished I could write poetry like that—but...

So I would settle for half as good...Do you know how good half as good as Clark Ashton Smith is? But that's enough of egotism.

What I do write is readable, and occasionally I manage a damn good one. Each one of the few friends who already took a peek at this little gathering have their own favourites, and I have mine, so I'll let you choose your own. If you don't like any of them, write to Jon Harvey*. If you do like them, buy me a brandy next time you see me, I reckon that's a fair deal.

As to the contents, there are SF poems for those of you who take your verse with a sprinkle of space-dust; heroic fantasy for all you S&S freaks; darkly macabre things for those who prefer a slightly more subtle approach and, of course, straight horror for those who like their meat red and preferably screaming. And there's at least one piece, *The Sea*, which isn't weird at all.

Looking at these poems again, it suddenly dawns on me that I know what they are—stories I never got round to writing in full. And those of them which look unfinished: they're the ones I hadn't quite worked out yet.

Damn! There must be two or three whole books full of stories here! And what did you pay for them?

As little as that?

How can you lose? It hardly makes it worthwhile to offer the usual warning—but I will, just for good measure:

Caveat Emptor, Baby!

Brian Lumley

*Jon Harvey is now deceased.

About the Author

Born in County Durham, he joined the British Army's Royal Military Police and wrote stories in his spare time before retiring with the rank of Warrant Officer Class 2 in 1980 and becoming a professional writer.

In the 1970s he added to H. P. Lovecraft's Cthulhu Mythos cycle of stories, including several tales and a novel featuring the character Titus Crow. Several of his early books were published by Arkham House. Other stories pastiched Lovecraft's Dream Cycle but featured Lumley's original characters David Hero and Eldin the Wanderer. Lumley once explained the difference between his Cthulhu Mythos characters and Lovecraft's: "My guys fight back. Also, they like to have a laugh along the way."

Later works included the Necroscope® series of novels, which produced spin-off series such as the Vampire World Trilogy, *The Lost Years* parts 1 and 2, and the E-Branch trilogy. The central protagonist of the earlier Necroscope® novels appears in the anthology *Harry Keogh and Other Weird Heroes*. The latest entry in the Necroscope saga is *The Möbius Murders*.

Lumley served as president of the Horror Writers Association from 1996 to 1997. In March 2010, Lumley was awarded Lifetime Achievement Award of the Horror Writers Association. He also received a World Fantasy Award for Lifetime Achievement in 2010.

Bibliography

Psychomech Trilogy
Psychomech
Psychosphere
Psychamok

Necroscope® Series
Necroscope
Necroscope II: Wamphyri!
Necroscope III: The Source
Necroscope IV: Deadspeak
Necroscope V: Deadspawn
Vampire World I: Blood Brothers
Vampire World II: The Last Aerie
Vampire World III: Bloodwars
Necroscope: The Lost Years, Volume I
Necroscope: The Lost Years, Volume II
Necroscope: Invaders
Necroscope: Defilers
Necroscope: Avengers
Harry Keogh: Necroscope & Other Weird Heroes
Necroscope: The Touch
Necroscope: The Möbius Murders

Dreamland Series
Hero of Dreams
Ship of Dreams
Mad Moon of Dreams

Iced on Aran

The House of Cthulhu
The House of Doors
The House of the Temple
The Last Rite
The Nonesuch and Others
The Plague-Bearer
The Return of the Deep Ones and Other Mythos Tales
The Second Wish and Other Exhalations
The Taint and Other Novellas
The Transition of Titus Crow
The Whisperer and Other Voices

Curious about other Crossroad Press books? Stop by our
website: http://crossroadpress.com
We offer quality writing
in digital, audio, and print formats.

Subscribe to our newsletter on the website homepage and receive
a free eBook.

www.ingramcontent.com/pod-product-compliance
Lightning Source LLC
Chambersburg PA
CBHW022048170626
46808CB00003B/1401